JOHNNY CROW'S GARDEN

WARNE CLASSICS SERIES

JOHNNY CROW'S GARDEN

L. LESLIE BROOKE

FREDERICK WARNE

FREDERICK WARNE

Penguin Books Ltd, Harmondsworth, Middlesex, England
Viking Penguin Inc., 40 West 23rd Street, New York, New York 10010, U.S.A.
Penguin Books Australia Ltd, Ringwood, Victoria, Australia
Penguin Books Canada Limited, 2801 John Street, Markham, Ontario, Canada L3R 1B4

First published 1903
Reprinted 1904, 1908, 1911, 1912, 1915, 1917, 1920,
1922, 1923, 1924, 1925, 1926, 1927, 1928, 1929, 1930,
1932, 1935, 1938, 1941, 1942, 1944, 1946, 1949, 1950,
1951, 1954, 1956, 1958, 1959, 1961,
1962, 1963, 1965, 1967 and 1968

This re-set edition published 1986

ISBN 0 7232 3429 9

Typeset by CCC, printed and bound in Great Britain by
William Clowes Limited, Beccles and London

To the Memory of my Father, who first told me of Johnny Crow's Garden, and to my Boys, for whom I have set on record these facts concerning it.

JOHNNY CROW'S
GARDEN

Johnny Crow
Would dig and sow

Till he made a little Garden.

And the Lion

Had a green and yellow Tie on

In Johnny Crow's Garden.

And the Rat
Wore a Feather in his Hat

But the Bear
Had nothing to wear

In Johnny Crow's Garden.

So the Ape

Took his Measure with a Tape

In Johnny Crow's Garden.

Then the Crane

Was caught in the Rain

In Johnny Crow's Garden.

And the Beaver
Was afraid he had a Fever

But the Goat
Said:

"It's nothing but his Throat!"

In Johnny Crow's Garden.

And the Pig
Danced a Jig

In Johnny Crow's Garden.

Then the Stork
Gave a Philosophic Talk

Till the Hippopotami
Said: "Ask no further 'What am I?'"

While the Elephant
Said something quite irrelevant

In Johnny Crow's Garden.

And the Goose—
Well,

the Goose *was* a Goose

The sign reads:

...ARE KINDLY
...QUESTED TO
...EP OFF THE
GRASS
J. Crow

In Johnny Crow's Garden.

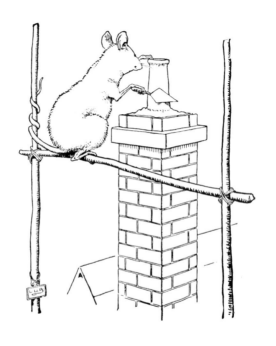

And the Mouse

Built himself a little House

Where the Cat

Sat down beside the Mat

In Johnny Crow's Garden.

And the Whale

Told a very long Tale

In Johnny Crow's Garden.

And the Owl
Was a funny old Fowl

And the Fox

Put them all in the Stocks

In Johnny Crow's Garden.

But Johnny Crow
He let them go

And they all sat down
to their dinner in a row

In Johnny Crow's Garden.

"GOOD-BYE!"

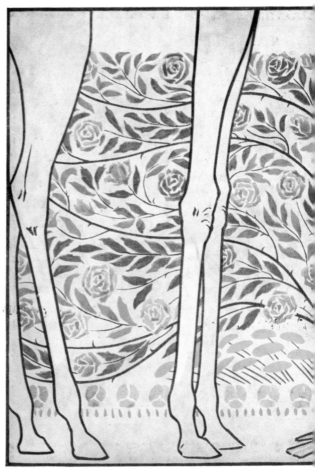